BEST FRIENDS
THINK ALIKE

by LYNN REISER

 Greenwillow Books, New York

FOR BETSY!

Sharpie and Crayola markers were used
to create the full-color art. The text type
is Swiss 721 Black.

Printed in Singapore by Tien Wah Press
First Edition 10 9 8 7 6 5 4 3 2 1

Library of Congress
Cataloging-in-Publication Data
Reiser, Lynn.
Best friends think alike / by Lynn Reiser.
      p.   cm.
Summary: Two best friends have a brief
disagreement, but then decide that playing
together is better than having your own way
alone.
ISBN 0-688-15199-X (trade)
ISBN 0-688-15200-7 (lib. bdg.)
[1. Friendship—Fiction.   2. Play—Fiction.]
I. Title.   PZ7.R27745Bg   1997
[E]—dc20   96-25924   CIP   AC

PLAY
IN ONE
AFTERNOON

CAST OF CHARACTERS
STARRING

 **RUBY—Beryl's best friend**

BERYL—Ruby's best friend

 **RUBY and BERYL
together**

SUPPORTING PLAYERS

Ruby's mother  **Ruby's father**

Beryl's mother  **Beryl's father**

**Ruby, it is time to go to the park.
What are you doing?**

**What are you doing, Beryl?
Are you ready to go to the park?**

I am thinking.
I am thinking of
a game to play in the park
with Beryl.

I am thinking.
I am thinking of
a game to play in the park
with Ruby.

**Hey,
Beryl!**

**Hey,
Ruby!**

I thought of
a game.

I thought of
a game,
too!

I thought of
horse and rider.

I thought of
horse and rider,
too!

It's the same game!

Best friends think alike!

The horse will be wild—
and the horse will know tricks.
The rider will wear
ruffles and ribbons—
and the rider will wear
a big hat and tall boots.

The horse will neigh
and stamp its feet.
The rider will hold the reins
and yell "Giddy-up!"
The horse will gallop,
and the rider will wave,
and—

**I thought of being the horse.
You can be the rider.**

But I thought of the horse.
You be the rider.

I, the horse—
You, the rider!

No.
YOU, the rider—
I, the horse!

I will not play with you.
I will be the wild horse
by myself!

I will not play with you,
either.
I will be the tricky horse
by myself!

But a horse needs a rider—

**to hold the reins
and yell "Giddy-up."**

I will be
the horse
AND
the rider
all by myself.

I will be
the horse
AND
the rider
all by myself.

BUT I WANTED

YO

TO PLAY WITH

U !

**Ruby, I thought of
a new game.**

**Beryl, I thought of
a new game, too!
I thought of
horses and riders!**

**I thought of
horses and riders, too!**

You can be
a horse and a rider—

and you can be
a horse and a rider.

It's

the same game!

We will

stamp our feet
      and neigh
and hold the reins
      and yell "Giddy-up"

and gallop
and wave—

TOGETHER!

**Beryl,
Ruby,
it's time
to go home.**

Ruby, what did you do today?

I played
horses and riders
with Beryl.
We thought of
the same game.

What did you do today, Beryl?

I played
horses and riders
with Ruby.
We thought of
the same game.

Best friends
think alike.